MYSTIC
™

SIEGE OF SCALES

Mystic: Volume 3: Siege of Scales

Publisher's Cataloging in Publication Data

  Mystic. Volume three : siege of scales / Writer: Ron Marz, Tony Bedard ; Penciler: Brandon Peterson ; Inker: John Dell ; Colorist: Andrew Crossley.

    p. : ill. ; cm.

  Spine title: Mystic. 3 : siege of scales

  ISBN: 1-931484-24-4

1. Fantasy fiction. 2. Adventure fiction. 3. Graphic novels. 4. Villard, Genevieve (Fictitious character) 4. Villard, Giselle (Fictitious character) I. Marz, Ron. II. Bedard, Tony. III. Peterson, Brandon. IV. Dell, John. V. Crossley, Andrew. VI. Title: Siege of scales VI. Title: Mystic. 3 : siege of scales.

PN6728 .M97 2002
813.54 [Fic]

MYSTIC™

SIEGE OF SCALES

Ron **MARZ** / Tony **BEDARD**
WRITERS

Brandon **PETERSON**
PENCILER

John **DELL**
INKER

Andrew **CROSSLEY**
COLORIST

CHAPTER 17
Fabrizio **FIORENTINO** · PENCILER
Matt **RYAN** · INKER
Elizabeth **LEWIS** · COLORIST

CHAPTER 19
Brandon **PETERSON** · PENCILER
Joe **WEEMS** / Matt **RYAN** · INKERS
Chris **GARCIA** / Mike **GARCIA** · COLORISTS

CHAPTER 20
Brandon **Peterson** · PENCILER
Joe **WEEMS** / Matt **RYAN** · INKERS
Chris **GARCIA** / Mike **GARCIA** · COLORISTS

Troy **PETERI** · LETTERER

COVER ART BY: Brandon Peterson

CrossGeneration Comics   **Oldsmar, Florida**

SIEGE OF SCALES

features
issues 15-20
from the ongoing series
MYSTIC

CIRESS

is a planet where magic reigns supreme.
For centuries the world has been ruled by
the seven major Guilds, or schools, of magic,
each presided over by a Guild Master. Each respective
Master serves as the living receptacle for an eternal spirit
embodying that particular Guild's sorcerous knowledge.

Despite her family's ties to the Nouveau Guild, socialite Giselle
Villard's disinterest in magic bordered on disdain. However,
Giselle's older sister Genevieve dutifully applied herself to magical
studies and stood poised to become Master of the Nouveau Guild.
But at Gen's Rite of Ascension, Giselle's palm was imprinted with
a mysterious sigil that somehow trapped the eternal spirits of all
seven Guilds within her. Granted vast magical might, Giselle
defeated the Masters in a battle for control of the spirits and
became the most powerful Mystic her world has ever known.

Refusing to accept defeat, the Masters summoned an entity
powerful enough to destroy Giselle – Animora, a creature who
had nearly conquered Ciress centuries before. However, Giselle
bested Animora, her sigil draining Animora's might from her.

Giselle imprisoned Animora on the spirit plane and returned to
strike a truce with the Guild Masters: Giselle secretly would retain
the eternal spirits, but the Masters would maintain their political
power. Now, with her talking squit Skitter as her companion,
Giselle faces her future…

GISELLE

GENEVIEVE

THIERRY

SKITTER

CHAPTER 15

I MEAN THE PICTURE, NOT THE...

SAME OLD SAME OLD. JUST ANOTHER NIGHT WITH THE USUAL CROWD.

YOU KNOW, *GISELLE* USED TO BE A REGULAR IN HERE, TOO. BUT IT'S BEEN A WHILE SINCE I'VE SEEN HER.

ALWAYS SEEMED A LITTLE FLIGHTY, THOUGH.

STILL, WOULD'VE BEEN NICE TO GET TO KNOW HER.

THERE ARE MORE SPRITES IN THE ETHER, THIERRY.

THAT'S WHAT THEY SAY.

SHOULD'VE REALIZED SOMEONE LIKE HER AND SOMEONE LIKE ME DIDN'T STAND MUCH CHANCE OF CONNECTING.

I GUESS WE'LL ALWAYS HAVE EACH OTHER, RIGHT ALPHONSE?

ALP

GROWF

Oh WELL...

...I'LL JUST FIND ANOTHER SUBJECT TO PAINT.

THIERRY?

I WAS HOPING I'D FIND YOU...

BRF?

APOLOGY ACCEPTED THEN.

WHAT ABOUT THAT GUY YOU WERE WITH? DARROW?

THAT DIDN'T WORK OUT. HE TURNED OUT TO BE...

...uh, TOO OLD FOR ME.

LOOK, THIERRY, I KNOW YOU HAVE NO REASON TO EVEN TALK TO ME, MUCH LESS BE MY FRIEND...

...OR ANYTHING ELSE...

...BUT I WAS HOPING WE COULD START FROM SCRATCH AND SEE WHERE THINGS GO.

YOU SEEM LIKE SUCH A NICE GUY, AND TO TELL YOU THE TRUTH, I'VE HAD MY SHARE OF PROBLEMS *FINDING* NICE GUYS.

OKAY...

...LOOK, DON'T TAKE THIS THE WRONG WAY, AND I'M NOT ASKING FOR AN EXPLANATION, BUT FOR WHATEVER REASON YOU *DID* ACT PRETTY WEIRD.

HOW CAN I BE SURE THAT'S NOT GOING TO HAPPEN AGAIN?

Ah.

THAT.

TO BE HONEST, I CAN'T GUARANTEE THINGS WON'T GET... *WEIRD*...ONCE IN A WHILE.

BECAUSE OF *THIS*. YOU WERE THERE JUST AFTER I GOT IT, REMEMBER?

RIGHT, BUT...WHAT IS IT?

WELCOME TO THE TANTRIC CATHEDRAL, GUILD MASTER VILLARD.

IF I CAN BE OF SERVICE TO YOU IN *ANY* WAY, PLEASE DON'T HESITATE TO ASK.

UH, NO... I'M FINE, THANKS.

FINE.

BUT IF I THINK OF ANYTHING I'LL... BE SURE TO LET YOU KNOW.

PLEASE DO.

FOLLOW ME.

ALL THE OTHER MASTERS HAVE ARRIVED AND AWAIT YOU WITHIN THE INNER SANCTUM.

WE OF THE TANTRIC GUILD FIND IT BEST WHEN THERE IS A WILLINGNESS TO CONJOIN FROM ALL PARTIES INVOLVED.

I HOPE YOUR DISCUSSIONS ARE FRUITFUL.

THANK YOU, I HOPE SO AS WELL.

FASHIONABLY LATE, I SEE.

FASHIONABLY *LOST*, VASHUA...

...BUT ONLY BRIEFLY.

SERVERS ARE DISMISSED.

PLEASE LEAVE US.

ALL OF YOUR ACOLYTES SEEM TO BE SUCH...

...HEALTHY...

...SPECIMENS.

THEN I'M GLAD YOU FOUND YOUR WAY. WE SHOULD BEGIN.

WE OF THE TANTRIC TAKE *PRIDE* IN OUR *OWN* BODIES AND *PLEASURE* IN THOSE OF OTHERS.

OBVIOUSLY.

THANK YOU FOR ALLOWING THIS TO TAKE PLACE HERE. THE NOUVEAU CATHEDRAL IS STILL A PILE OF RUBBLE UNFORTUNATELY.

THIS WAS THE ONLY SITE UPON WHICH ALL SEVEN OF US COULD AGREE.

PLEASE, SIT.

A SHREWD TACTIC, MAKING US *WAIT* FOR YOU, GENEVIEVE. PERHAPS YOU HAVE THE MAKINGS OF A GUILD MASTER AFTER ALL.

AND PERHAPS YOU ASCRIBE TO ME DUPLICITY TO WHICH *YOU* WOULD BE MORE PRONE, MAGUS.

THE PEOPLE ARE IGNORANT THAT EACH OF US IS AN EMPTY VESSEL. THEY WON'T KNOW THE TRUTH...

...BECAUSE THEY *CAN'T* KNOW THE TRUTH. THE SECRET MUST NEVER BE REVEALED, AND WE SEVEN MUST COMPEL EACH OTHER TO KEEP IT.

WHAT RIGHT HAVE *YOU* TO MAKE DEMANDS?!

YOU ACT AS IF YOU'RE IN A POSITION TO *DICTATE*, RATHER THAN BEING ONE WHO IS BARELY AN EQUAL!

IT *IS* TIME WE DEVOTED OURSELVES TO RULING OUR DOMAINS RATHER THAN THIS INCESSANT SQUABBLING.

PARTICULARLY NOW, WHILE WE CAN TAKE ADVANTAGE OF THE POPULAR SUPPORT WE REAPED FROM ANIMORA'S DEFEAT.

ZAI?

AGREED.

YINMA?

WHAT OTHER OPTION IS LEFT?

MAGUS?

YES, DAMN YOU.

YES.

GOOD.

...*NORMAL* MEANING I'M SUPPOSED TO BE THE MAGICAL PROTECTOR OF CIRESS.

LOOK, IF THIS IS TOO WEIRD FOR YOU, IT'S OKAY.

I'LL BRING YOU BACK TO JAZZRAT'S OR WHEREVER YOU WANT TO GO.

NO, I THINK I'M OKAY WITH IT. I *THINK.*

THEN YOU'LL *STAY* A LITTLE WHILE?

SURE, I CAN'T WAIT TO SEE WHAT HAPPENS NEXT.

SORRY THE PLACE IS SUCH A MESS. MY APARTMENT'S PROBABLY A LITTLE WORSE, IF YOU CAN BELIEVE IT.

I REALLY NEED TO CLEAN ALL THIS UP AND FIGURE OUT WHAT'S HERE, BUT...

...WELL, TIDINESS WAS NEVER MY FORTÉ.

TRUTHFULLY, I HAVEN'T EVEN EXPLORED MOST OF IT. WANT TO HAVE A LOOK AROUND WITH ME?

WITH THE MAGICAL PROTECTOR OF CIRESS TO KEEP ME SAFE...

...HOW CAN I REFUSE?

WE'RE GOING FOR A WALK. YOU COMING?

NAH, TOO MUCH EFFORT. IF IT'S ALL THE SAME TO YOU, I'LL STAY HERE AND MAKE ALPHONSE NERVOUS.

SUIT YOURSELF.

THE. SQUIT. TALKS.

I'VE GOTTEN USED TO IT.

BELIEVE ME, WITH EVERYTHING ELSE THAT'S HAPPENED, A TALKING SQUIT DOESN'T SEEM LIKE THAT BIG A DEAL ANYMORE.

HANG ON, I SHOULD AT LEAST TIDY THIS UP.

THIS MAGIC STUFF *DOES* HAVE ITS USES.

SKRAKAKRAK

COULDN'T YOU JUST REBUILD THE NOUVEAU CATHEDRAL LIKE THAT?

PROBABLY...

...BUT I KNOW THAT'S SOMETHING GEN WANTS TO TAKE CARE OF HERSELF.

SHE SEEMS NICE, YOUR SISTER. IT'S OBVIOUS HOW MUCH SHE CARES ABOUT YOU.

GEN PRACTICALLY RAISED ME.

OUR RELATIONSHIP'S HAD ITS ROCKY PATCHES, BUT NOW IT'S THE BEST IT'S *EVER* BEEN.

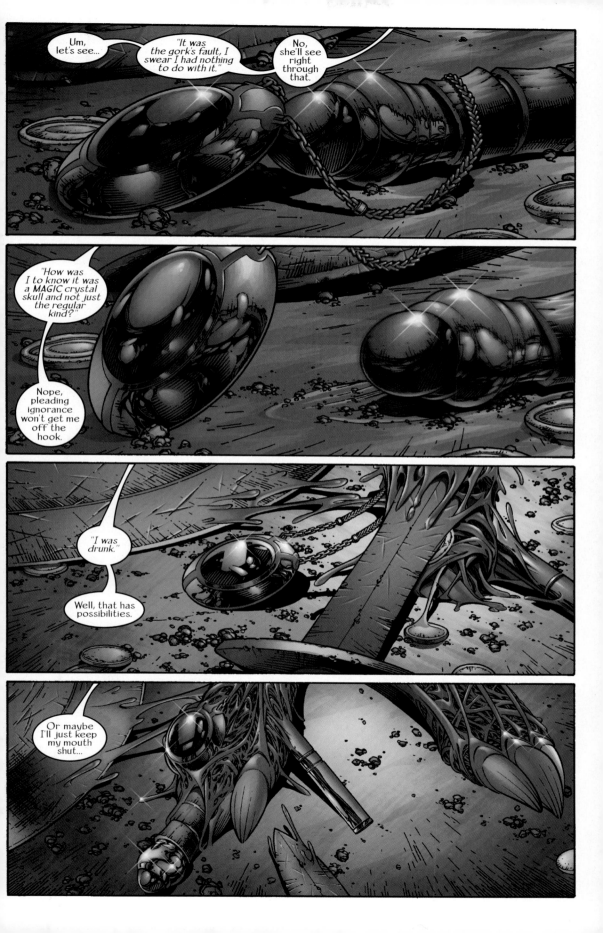

CHAPTER 16

WHERE DID IT COME FROM, GEN?

I HAVEN'T A CLUE. I'VE NEVER SEEN ANYTHING LIKE IT.

COULD IT HAVE FOLLOWED YOU HERE SOMEHOW?

I DON'T SEE HOW. ALL THE WARDS WE PUT IN PLACE AROUND THE MOON ARE STILL THERE.

THE ONLY ONES WHO CAN GET IN AND OUT OF HERE ARE ME AND YOU.

IT WAS LIKE A *PATCHWORK*, JUST BITS AND PIECES.

WHATEVER IT WAS, SEEMS LIKE IT'S ALL OVER...

...OR NOT.

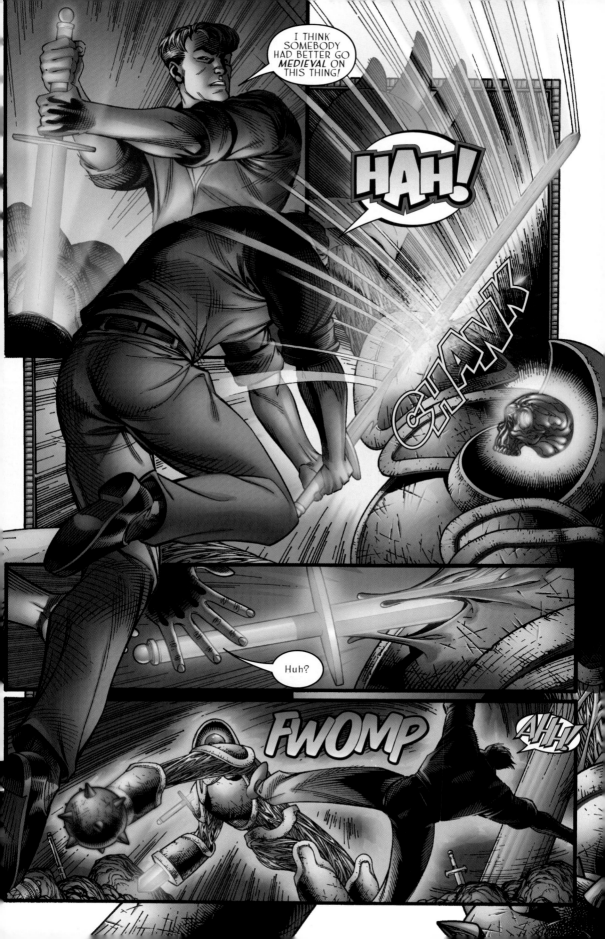

YOU'RE SWEET...

UFF!

...BUT STAY OUT OF THE WAY AND LEAVE THIS TO THE GIRLS, OKAY?

OOOOH

WHATEVER YOU SAY.

ANY IDEAS?

MAYBE SOME KIND OF AMBUSH LEFT BEHIND BY THE GUILD MASTERS?

POSSIBLY, BUT I DOUBT IT. IT DOESN'T EVEN STRIKE ME AS SENTIENT, IT'S MORE LIKE SOME KIND OF GOLEM.

IT'S JUST ABSORBING WHATEVER'S AROUND IT...

...MAKING ITSELF *BIGGER* ALL THE TIME.

ALL RIGHT, IF IT'S FEEDING OFF THE ARTIFACTS IN HERE...

...WE'LL JUST TAKE *IT* AWAY FROM THE ARTIFACTS.

THAT SHOULD AT LEAST STOP IT FROM GROWING.

WHAT ABOUT THE ETERNAL SPIRITS, 'ELLE? ANY WORD FROM THEM?

HEY, YOU GUYS *ARE* PRETTY QUIET.

ANY POINTERS?

HELLO?

SHRUKK

APOLOGIES FOR OUR SILENCE, GISELLE, BUT THIS CREATURE IS UNKNOWN TO ANY OF US.

WELL?

LOOKS LIKE IT'S JUST ME AND YOU.

SKRAKOOM

NOT BAD, 'ELLE.

ARE YOU *KIDDING*, NOT BAD? WE WIPED IT OUT! WE—

DO YOU... FEEL THAT?

I FEEL THAT.

DO YOU *SEE* THAT?

I SEE THAT...

SEE? IT'S NOT ABSORBING ANYTHING AROUND IT.

I THINK IT'S DEAD.

I HOPE.

SO WHAT DID YOU *DO*, EXACTLY?

EXACTLY?

I'M NOT REAL SURE. BUT I'M SURE IT *WASN'T* MAGIC. IT WAS....

...SOMETHING ELSE. LIKE RAW ENERGY CHANNELED THROUGH *THIS* SOMEHOW.

I DON'T KNOW WHERE IT CAME FROM, BUT IT'S NOT LIKE ANYTHING I'VE EVER FELT BEFORE.

Wow, who ordered WELL DONE?

LOOK WHO DECIDES TO SHOW UP NOW THAT IT'S *SAFE*.

YOU AND I ARE GOING TO HAVE A LONG TALK ABOUT THINGS, FURBALL.

What're you blaming me for? I'm just an innocent bystander.

SURE YOU ARE.

GISELLE!

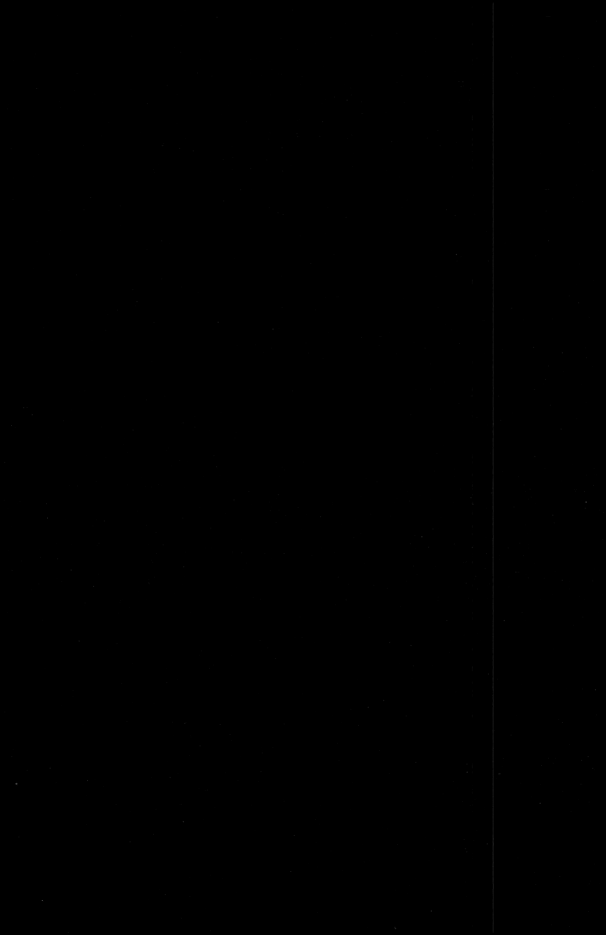

CHAPTER 17

SO WHAT DO WE HAVE TODAY, JULIAN?

THE MASTERS OF THREE ANCILLARY GUILDS ARE MAKING OFFICIAL VISITS.

THEY ARRIVED A SHORT TIME AGO AND I'VE ALREADY GREETED THEM.

THEY AWAIT YOU IN THE LeCAVALIER SANCTUARY.

YOU RECEIVED THE SCROLLS BRIEFING YOU AS TO THE INDIVIDUAL GUILDS AND MASTERS?

I DID.

OSTENSIBLY, OF COURSE, THEY'RE HERE TO PAY THEIR RESPECTS TO NOUVEAU'S NEW MASTER.

BUT THEY'RE CERTAINLY HOPING TO TAKE ADVANTAGE OF YOUR INEXPERIENCE AND IMPROVE THEIR RESPECTIVE ALLIANCES.

I KNOW YOU DON'T RELISH THE POLITICAL ASPECTS OF YOUR POSITION, GENEVIEVE...

...BUT THE SUPPORT OF THE ANCILLARY GUILDS IS A NECESSITY.

WE SHOULDN'T KEEP THEM WAITING.

ONLY A MOMENT LONGER, JULIAN.

"THERE'S ALWAYS TIME TO ADMIRE A BLOSSOM."

DO YOU KNOW WHO TAUGHT ME THAT WHEN I WAS JUST A GIRL?

I REMEMBER. BUT ARE YOU REMINDING ME THAT I'M OLD...

...OR THAT YOU WERE A GOOD STUDENT?

...MASTER SENGAL OF THE SAMEDI GUILD...

THANK YOU FOR RECEIVING ME.

...MASTER GUO OF THE DRAGON GUILD...

HONORED.

...AND MASTER SHAEDRA OF THE PROTEAN GUILD.

I'VE LOOKED FORWARD TO THIS MEETING FOR SOME TIME.

I TRUST WE CAN BUILD RELATIONSHIPS THAT WILL BE BENEFICIAL TO *ALL* OUR GUILDS. THERE ARE A GREAT MANY THINGS FOR US TO DISCUSS...

...BUT I THOUGHT WE MIGHT BEGIN WITH A TOUR OF THE CATHEDRAL.

WE WOULD BE MOST INTERESTED.

AS YOU SEE, WE'VE BEEN FORTUNATE ENOUGH TO RECOVER FROM THE DISASTER THAT CLAIMED OUR ORIGINAL STRUCTURE.

IMPRESSIVE.

I'M JUST PLEASED WE WERE ABLE TO RESTORE THE TRUE HEART OF OUR GUILD.

YOU BARGAINED WITH THE EQUAR ARCHITECTS, DID YOU NOT?

...ID.

IT WAS A... MUTUALLY BENEFICIAL AGREEMENT.

THEN YOU *DO* UNDERSTAND THE IMPORTANCE...

...OF MAINTAINING...

...A NETWORK OF ALLIANCES.

I TRUST YOUR REGIME WILL NOT UNDERESTIMATE HOW *USEFUL* THE SUPPORT OF GUILDS SUCH AS OURS CAN BE IN THE POLITICAL STRUGGLES OF CIRESS.

I ASSURE YOU, MASTER GUO, I VALUE THE AID OF THE ANCILLARY GUILDS.

LET US HOPE. FOR TOO LONG THE CONTRIBUTIONS OF MY PARTICULAR GUILD HAVE BEEN TAKEN FOR GRANTED.

IT WOULD BE MOST TRAGIC IF THIS WERE TO REMAIN UNCHANGED.

KEEP AN EYE ON THAT ONE. HE CONCERNS ME.

YES, SIR.

NOUVEAU HAS A LONG TRADITION OF EQUITABLE RELATIONSHIPS WITH THE ANCILLARIES.

I HAVE NO INTENTION OF CHANGING THAT POLICY.

WE THREE...

...SAMEDI, DRAGON, PROTEAN...

...COULD FORM A POWERFUL BLOCK IF ALIGNED WITH **ANY ONE** OF THE MAJOR GUILDS.

FIRST WE LISTEN TO WHAT NOUVEAU HAS TO OFFER.

THOUGH I **WOULD** BE MORE COMFORTABLE HAVING SUCH DISCUSSIONS IN A PRIVATE SETTING.

OF COURSE.

WE CAN CONTINUE OUR CONVERSATION IN THE GARDENS. THEY'VE ALWAYS BEEN MY FAVORITE ASPECT OF THE CATHEDRAL.

JULIAN, IF YOU AND THE GUARDS WOULD LEAVE US FOR A TIME?

I'M NOT SURE BEING ALONE WITH THEM IS THE WISEST CHOICE, MASTER VILLARD.

AT LEAST PERMIT *ME* TO ACCOMPANY—

THEY'RE OUR *GUESTS*, JULIAN. IT'S FINE.

I HOPE THAT'S TRUE.

NOW...

...YOU HAVE ME ALL TO YOURSELVES.

PLEASE, SPEAK CANDIDLY.

BEAR IN MIND, MASTER VILLARD, WE SPEAK NOT SOLELY FOR OURSELVES, BUT FOR *ALL* THE ANCILLARY GUILDS.

YOUR ASCENSION IS BEING VIEWED AS AN OPPORTUNITY TO CORRECT THE INJUSTICES OF THE PAST.

IT'S HOPED *YOU* WILL HAVE THE COURAGE TO BE AN AGENT OF CHANGE.

THE ATTACKER CHOSE TO *PERISH* RATHER THAN BE TAKEN.

TO KEEP US FROM LEARNING THE TRUTH BEHIND THE ASSASSINATION PLOT.

WHAT OF THE OTHER MASTERS?

WE ARE NOT TO BLAME!

I ASSURE YOU, WE KNEW *NOTHING* OF THIS.

RELEASE THEM.

IT'S OBVIOUS WE'VE *ALL* BEEN THE VICTIMS OF DUPLICITY.

YES, BUT *WHOSE?*

THAT'S WHAT CONCERNS ME MOST, JULIAN. WE HAVE AN ENEMY OUT THERE...

...AND NO IDEA WHO IT IS.

FINE. I'M FINE, EVERYTHING'S OKAY... ...BUT I'M TRUTHFULLY TOO EXHAUSTED TO EVEN TALK ABOUT IT RIGHT NOW.

WHAT ABOUT YOUR DAY?

LESS EXCITING THAN *YOURS*. I SPENT IT WITH THIERRY, LOOKING IN THE ART GALLERIES DOWN BY THE WATERFRONT.

YOU KNOW, 'ELLE, *I* WAS THE ONE WHO WANTED THE RESPONSIBILITY. I WORKED TO *GET* IT. NOW...

...SOMETIMES IT FEELS LIKE SUCH A BIG WEIGHT TO SHOULDER ALL THE TIME.

EVEN WHEN I DIDN'T *WANT* YOU TO BE, YOU WERE THERE FOR ME, GEN.

HERE...

...YOU KNOW WHOSE SHOULDER YOU CAN ALWAYS LEAN ON.

MOMO?

AGAIN, MOMO.

SURE, BOSS. I'M RIGHT HERE.

HOW *AMUSED* INGRA WOULD BE TO SEE ME REDUCED TO THIS STATE, AND THESE WRETCHED SURROUNDINGS.

AND ALL BECAUSE OF A *WOMAN*.

SOON, THOUGH...

...SOON I'LL BE WHOLE AGAIN.

HELP ME UP.

YOU *SURE*, BOSS? I MEAN, YOU'RE NOT EXACTLY IN GREAT SHAPE.

IT WASN'T A REQUEST.

WE WERE SIMPLY UNPREPARED, ANIMORA AND I. WE DIDN'T UNDERSTAND THE EXTENT OF THE SIGIL'S POWER.

JACKET.

THAT'S A MISTAKE I'LL NOT MAKE AGAIN.

I CERTAINLY CAN'T GO BACK TO ELYSIA AND THE FIRST.

BUT IF THE RUMORS ARE TRUE...

...THEN ANIMORA WAS IMPRISONED ON THE SPIRIT PLANE RATHER THAN DESTROYED.

SO WHAT ARE YOU GOING TO DO, BOSS?

I'M GOING TO *FREE* HER...

...AND TOGETHER WE'LL REAP OUR VENGEANCE ON THIS MISERABLE PLANET *AND* GISELLE VILLARD.

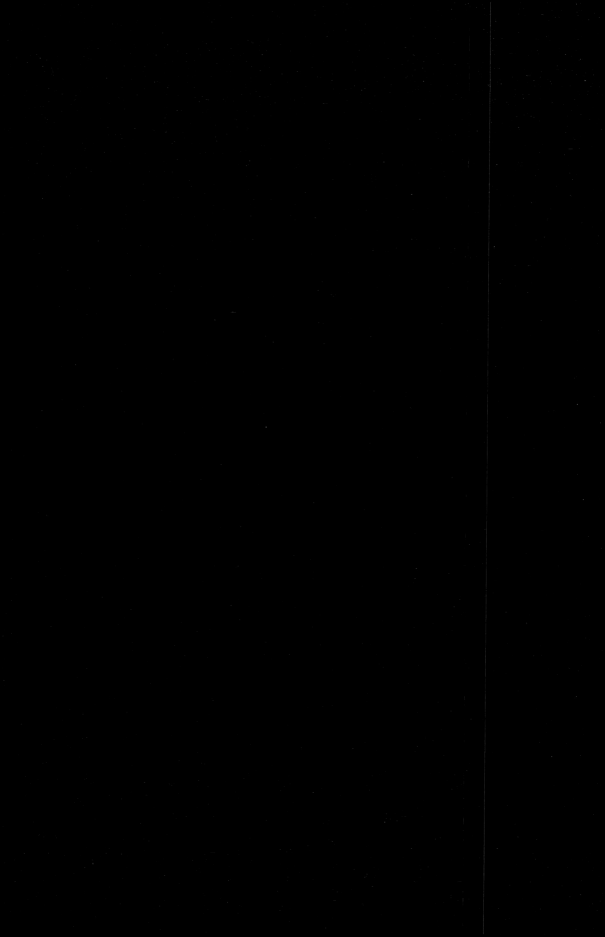

CHAPTER 18

BESIDES, SINCE I HAVE TO KEEP A LOW PROFILE, WHO ELSE WILL GET THE DOOR?

SOMEONE HERE, BOSS? I DIDN'T HEAR THE BELL.

NOT *THAT* DOOR...

EVERYTHING HAS ITS *PRICE*, MOMO. *TRAVEL*, IN PARTICULAR, CAN TAX ONE'S RESOURCES.

I'M LUCKY THESE FINE GENTLEMEN COULD PAY MY WAY, SINCE I'M NOT EXACTLY FLUSH THESE DAYS.

THEIR KINDNESS WILL BE FONDLY REMEMBERED.

BE A PET AND SNAP THEIR NECKS BEFORE THEY WAKE UP?

MERCI.

NO OFFENSE, GISELLE, BUT THANKS FOR LEAVING THE SQUIT AT HOME.

NONE TAKEN. I DIDN'T WANT SKITTER DISTRACTING YOU.

SO, YOU ACTUALLY DO ALL THIS STUFF *BY HAND?* NO MAGICAL SHORTCUTS?

NOPE. FOR BETTER OR WORSE, THAT'S ALL *ME.*

I TRY TO KEEP SWITCHING *MEDIA.* OIL PAINT, PASTELS, CLAY, MARBLE. THE VARIETY KEEPS THINGS FRESH.

DOESN'T LOOK LIKE THE *SUBJECT MATTER* CHANGES MUCH, THOUGH.

Huh?

NOTHING.

THIS IS THE *SPOT*, RIGHT?

RIGHT.

THIERRY, I GOTTA ADMIT... AT FIRST, I WASN'T SURE I COULD *DO* THIS. I MEAN, A GIRL COULD FEEL, Y'KNOW... VULNERABLE, TO SAY THE LEAST.

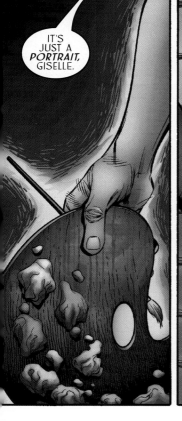

IT'S JUST A *PORTRAIT,* GISELLE.

DON'T WORRY. IN ABOUT TEN MINUTES YOU'LL GO FROM NERVOUS TO *BORED.*

I KINDA *DOUBT* THAT.

Huh?

...**WHOA!**

BUT... ALL YOUR *OTHER* WORK...

...YOUR *SKETCHES*...

...AND SINCE YOU PICKED *THIS* AS A BACKDROP, I ASSUMED...

I JUST... I WOULD *NEVER*...

WAIT. SHE OBVIOUSLY *LOATHES* THIS WORM. WHY WASTE A GOOD OPPORTUNITY?

NO!

DARLING, PLEASE...

GRAHH! YOU'VE *THROWN AWAY* MY LAST SHRED OF HOPE!

IF I HAD *ANY* STRENGTH LEFT, I'D *OBLITERATE* YOU!

THEN *KISS* ME, INSTEAD... AND TAKE *STRENGTH* FROM MY LOVE...

GET HIM *OFF* ME! GET HIM—

KRIK RMMMBLESH

--FROM ANIMORA?

er...

CHAPTER 19

≥ACK≤

ORACLE!

MASTER! WHAT *IS* THIS?

THE *LAST* THING YOU WILL EVER SEE IF YOU DON'T MOVE FAST!

WE ARE GOING TO NEED *HELP!* BUT MY DUTY IS TO STAND AND *FIGHT*...

YOU TAKE THIS TO THE *NOUVEAU* MASTER. IT HAS AN *ENTRY GLYPH* THAT WILL GUIDE YOU STRAIGHT TO HER.

...SURVIVORS FROM THE ENCHANTRESS CATHEDRAL SAID THE TENTACLES SHED SPECIAL *SCALES*--

--AND THAT THOSE SCALES SPROUTED UP INTO SEPARATE *CREATURES* THE MOMENT THEY FELL TO THE GROUND.

LIKE PLANTING *DRAGON'S TEETH.*

EXACTLY. I HAVE TWO DIVISIONS OF SCRY-CORPS WORKING ON A *COUNTER-SPELL.* NO JOY SO FAR...

MEANWHILE, SIMILAR INCURSIONS HAVE BEEN REPORTED IN *OTHER* GUILD LANDS, MOVING *UP* STEADILY FROM THE SOUTHERN LATITUDES.

THE SCALE-BEASTS HAVE MARCHED RIGHT THROUGH *EVERYTHING* THROWN AT THEM--THE DJINN ROC BOMBER WING, THE SHAMAN SPIRIT-DRUMMERS, THE TANTRIC CHI-CASTERS--

ARE YOU SUGGESTING WE CAN'T WIN, GENERAL LAURANCE?

YOU CAN SEE CLEARLY ENOUGH *WHO* WE'RE UP AGAINST, AND WE'VE BEATEN HER BEFORE...

IF YOU'RE IMPLYING THIS IS *ANIMORA'S* WORK, THEN I MUST HAVE *MISSED* A BRIEFING.

...BECAUSE *YOU* AND THE OTHER GUILD MASTERS ASSURED US SHE'S IN *CUSTODY* ON THE SPIRIT PLANE. *CORRECT?*

YES...WELL, APPARENTLY *NOT.*

NOW, WHAT ABOUT MY *SISTER?* HAVE YOUR MEN BROUGHT HER IN AS REQUESTED?

DON'T WORRY, THEY HAVE HER APARTMENT BUILDING SECURED. BUT YOU DON'T NEED HER *DISTRACTING* YOU RIGHT NOW.

DO NOT SECOND-GUESS ME! SOMEBODY BRING ME A *PHONE!*

MASTER VILLARD! STAY BEHIND—

STAND DOWN, JACQUES. SEE THAT GLYPH? IT'S THE HOTLINE SCROLL I GAVE TO MASTER YINMA.

GENEVIEVE VILLARD, MASTER OF THE NOUVEAU GUILD! THE DEMON QUEEN HAS *RETURNED!*

YOUR SISTER *MUST* KNOW HOW ANIMORA ESCAPED! ENLIST HER *AID!*

NOT *AGAIN* WITH YOUR SISTER! WITH ALL DUE RESPECT, HOW COULD A *DEBUTANTE* BE OF *ANY* USE TO US AT A TIME LIKE THIS?

LONG STORY. THE IMPORTANT THING RIGHT NOW IS THAT IT'S ONE-THIRTY IN THE *AFTERNOON*...

...SO THERE'S ONLY *ONE PLACE* GISELLE COULD BE...

RING RING

Hey!

...huh...?

It's about TIME, sleeping beauty! I was beginning to think I'd have to take MYSELF for a walk...

...only YOU tell me how I'm supposed to hold my own LEASH...!

YEAH, OKAY. LEMME GET DRESSED.

Mm...STILL CAN'T BELIEVE, AFTER EVERYTHING THAT HAPPENED BETWEEN US LAST NIGHT, HE DIDN'T ASK ME TO STAY OVER.

YOU DON'T THINK THERE'S SOMETHING *WRONG* WITH HIM, DO YOU?

Who, THIERRY? Not unless being a GENTLEMAN counts as "something wrong" nowadays.

RING RING

RING RING

Or haven't you ever MET a gentleman?

RING RING

Y'know, they even do things like CALL the next day...

GISELLE!

WH...?

COME TO US! NOW!

"...WHERE ARE THE *GUILD MASTERS* OF THE FALLEN LANDS?"

VERY IMPRESSIVE RESULTS, ANIMORA, BUT WHY THE *RUSH*? SOMEHOW, I EXPECTED YOU TO *SAVOR* THE CONQUEST...

WHY *BOTHER*? THIS WORLD MAY BE A *RICH* LITTLE MORSEL, BUT IT'S STILL JUST THE *APPETIZER*.

ARGUS ONE TO NOUVEAU LINE COMMAND! APPROACHING ENEMY FRONT! DO YOU COPY?

ROGER THAT, ARGUS...

...TROOPS ARE STANDING BY. HOW MANY UNITS SHOULD WE ACTIVATE, OVER?

ALL OF THEM! REPEAT, COMMIT ALL FORCES!

...AND THEN SEE IF YOU CAN CONJURE UP MORE...!

WE'RE HARDLY SLOWING THEM DOWN.

GENERAL CLEMENT, INFORM THE ACOLYTES: IT'S TIME TO ACTIVATE THE *COLOSSI.*

AYE, MASTER VILLARD.

GISELLE, WHERE *ARE* YOU...?

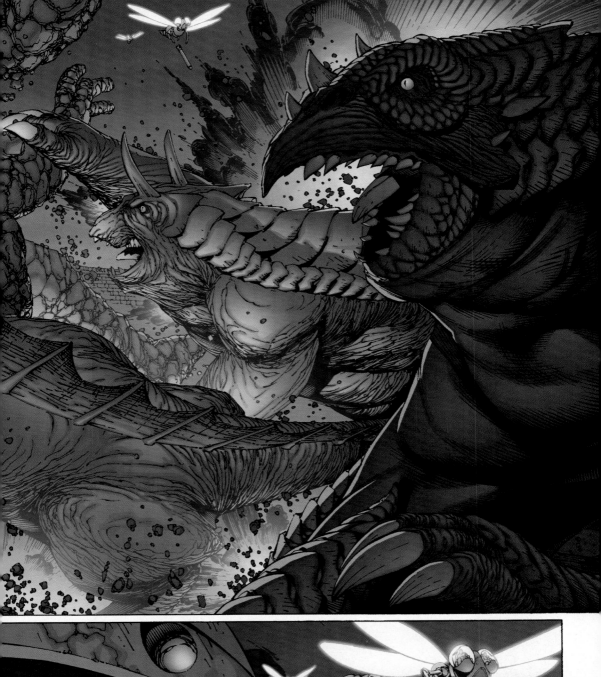

ONWARD!

HURRY, GISELLE...

MASTER! SOMEONE'S TELEPORTING IN!

MMMMMMM

FINALLY! IT'S OKAY! IT'S ONLY MY SIS--

--TER...?

FWASH

WHAT DOES IT TAKE... TO GET HER ATTENTION? WHY DOES SHE NOT... SHOW HER FACE?!

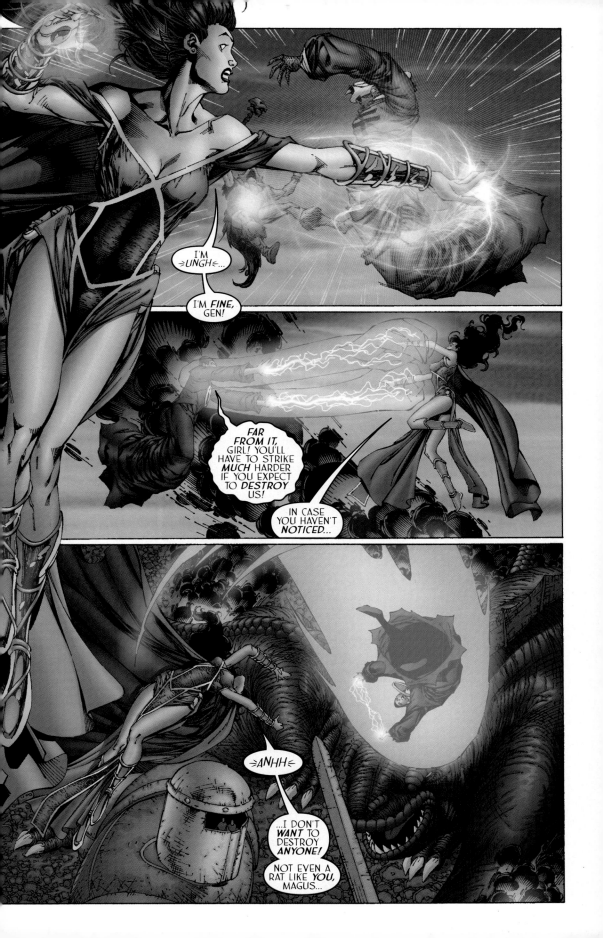

CHAPTER 20

GISELLE!

BAM

THRUNCH

COLOSSUS FIVE TO NOUVEAU LINE COMMAND! WE'VE TAKEN A HIT!

...WAIT ...→NGH←... DON'T...

THEY'VE SWITCHED FROM SPELL-CASTING TO MORE DIRECT PHYSICAL ATTACKS!

GISELLE, YOU CAN'T DEFLECT THESE LIKE THE OTHER—

CALM DOWN, LeCAVALIER. IF THEY'RE GETTING PHYSICAL WITH HER, THEN THEY'VE STRAYED INTO MY TERRITORY.

AND WHAT WOULD THE TANTRIC GUILD SUGGEST?

KISSING THE ENEMY? OR PERHAPS A NICE GROUP HUG?

THE SPELL I HAVE IN MIND WOULD REQUIRE GISELLE TO SHUNT MUCH OF HER POWER INTO A TOUGHER BODY...

WHOOSH

Eh?

⇒HAKK⇐

⇒UNGH⇐ YOU BOYS WANNA STEP *INSIDE?*

NO!

SHUK

SHHHH

FRANCOIS, DID YOU HAVE ANY *IDEA*--

--THAT THE GUILD MASTER'S *SISTER* COULD *DO* THIS KIND OF THING? *NONE.*

GUESS I WAS TOO BUSY STARING AT HER *LEGS,* LIKE EVERYONE ELSE.

GENTLEMEN... ⇒NFF⇐...IF YOU DON'T *MIND...*

SHE CAN *HEAR* US..?!

ANIMORA! HELP US!

SHHHLUK

GENERAL LAURANCE!

MASTER VILLARD.

GENEVIEVE...

I SERVED YOUR *FATHER.* I'VE *KNOWN* YOU AND GISELLE SINCE YOU WERE LITTLE GIRLS. *YOU* TURNED OUT TO BE EVERYTHING I EXPECTED... BUT *TELL* ME...

...WHAT IN THE WORLD HAS YOUR *SISTER* TURNED INTO...?

OUR LAST HOPE.

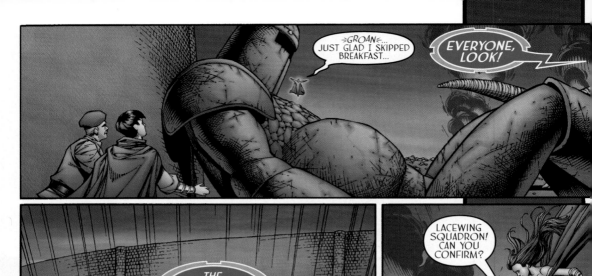

GROAN... JUST GLAD I SKIPPED BREAKFAST...

EVERYONE, LOOK!

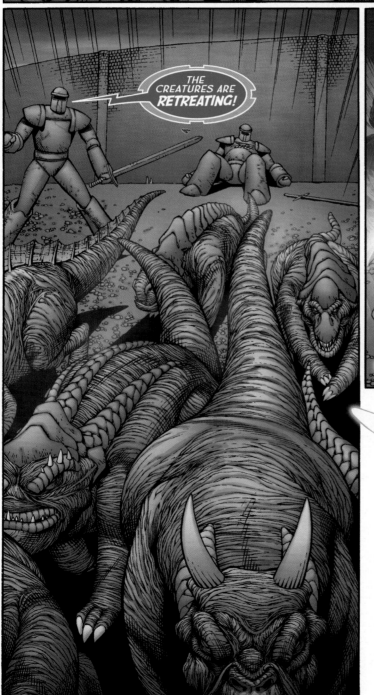

THE CREATURES ARE **RETREATING!**

LACEWING SQUADRON! CAN YOU CONFIRM?

LACEWING TWO HERE. THEY'RE NOT EXACTLY **RETREATING,** GENERAL...

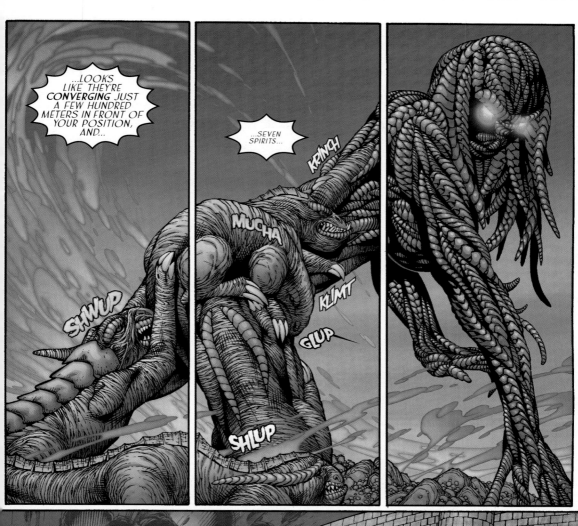

...LOOKS LIKE THEY'RE **CONVERGING** JUST A FEW HUNDRED METERS IN FRONT OF YOUR POSITION, AND...

...SEVEN SPIRITS...

KRINCH

MUCHA

SHWUP

KLIMT

GLUP

SHLUP

MASTER VILLARD...

I *SEE* IT, JACQUES.

Oh, THAT IS JUST **GROSS**...

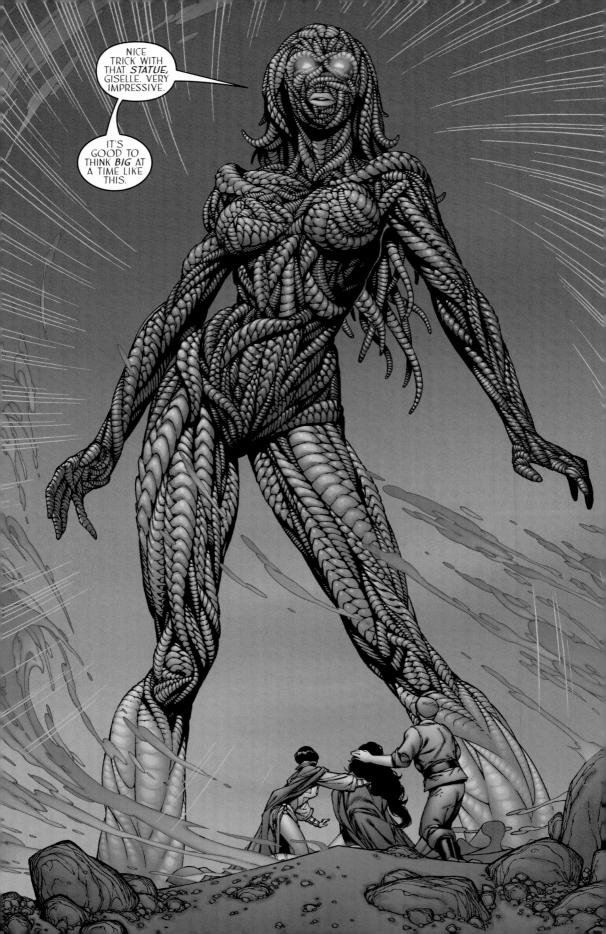

AND HOW YOU *LOVED* IT-- FEELING ME WITHER IN YOUR HANDS! WATCHING THE LIGHT FADE FROM MY EYES!

NO! ⇒NNF⇐... IT FELT *SICK!*

YES, YES...YOUR PRECIOUS *MORALITY.* IT MAKES YOU *BETTER* THAN ME, DOESN'T IT?

THAT KIND OF THINKING -- THAT *"RIGHT"* VERSUS *"WRONG" GIBBERISH* -- SPLIT MY PEOPLE IN TWO...

⇒ANH

SHHRIPPP

GET BEHIND ME.

...AND IF THERE'S *ONE THING* I'LL MAKE YOU SEE BEFORE YOU DIE--

--IT'S THAT MORALS MEAN *NOTHING* AGAINST *TRUE POWER!*

SPLUT

LAURANCE!

GEN!

ALL OF THIS...JUST TO GET HERSELF KILLED?

NO... THERE IS ANOTHER CASUALTY HERE...

GISELLE! GET AWAY FROM HER!

...YOU WIN...

...YOU WIN...

...YOU WIN...

MAKING THE COVER

WITH BRANDON PETERSON

When Ron Marz and I were designing the world of MYSTIC, we wanted to give Giselle and her Guild a distinctive look. For inspiration we looked to art nouveau, a style that originated in Paris and became a worldwide phenomenon by the 1920s. Art nouveau translates very easily to comics because it's a decorative style with a heavy emphasis on line work and flowing shapes and forms. It's also very beautiful.

My favorite artist of this period is Alphonse Mucha (1860-1939), who was one of the originators and masters of art nouveau. Mucha

JOB by Alphonse Mucha, 1896 (Image #1)

La Danse by Alphonse Mucha, 1898 (Image #2)

was primarily a commercial artist who painted for posters, print advertising, labels and packaging. His artwork is reminiscent of cartoons in that he would use bold clean outlines to contain color, so it spoke to me immediately as a comic book artist. I used that influence heavily the entire time I was drawing MYSTIC, and this trade paperback cover is the first time I was able to duplicate more of the pure technique that he and his contemporaries used.

Images #1-#3 are a fairly good example of Mucha's work. The borders are decorative, and this decoration is carried through to the center of the illustration. In fact, the decorative aspects are incorporated within the illustration — instead of being something around the illustration, they're part of it.

One thing I find attractive in Mucha's work is his use of long, flowing lines in hair and drapery. I also like his controlled and muted color scheme. These are aspects of his art that I enjoy but could never bring to the comic. For one thing, Mucha's palette was much more subdued and minimal than what is called for in an adventure comic like MYSTIC. Likewise, you can't use art nouveau decorative techniques in story pages, because they would interfere with the storytelling.

Covers are a different story. As this cover was my last MYSTIC artwork, I wanted to go out with a bang by recreating a pure art nouveau piece. The cover is my homage to Mucha. As a result, the color theory, design and even the anatomy of the character is reflective of his style.

I've been working with computers in one way or another since Adobe released Photoshop 1.0. Computers (and Photoshop) have gotten so powerful that it's now possible to "paint" digitally. This is a technique that I'm employing on my next CrossGen project, CHIMERA, which is completely computer-rendered. It was only natural to digitally paint this cover, especially since it's an homage to one of my favorite painters. Here's how I went about it.

Clair de Lune by Alphonse Mucha, 1902 (Image #3)

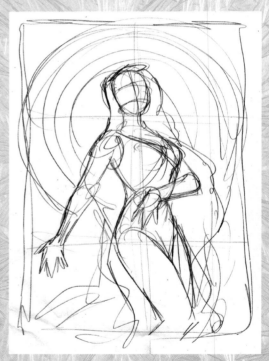

STEP ONE: THUMBNAIL

I always start with a small thumbnail drawing of the piece as a general guide. The thumbnail is usually no more than an eighth of the size of the final artwork, maybe three inches high. I roughly block in the major elements, which for this piece are the figure and the background design elements.

It's important to do a thumbnail before just jumping into the actual work. Once you've committed to a piece of art and are doing a finished drawing, it's very hard to think of the piece as a whole. Instead, you think of it in terms of all the little areas you focus on one by one. The danger is that you may lose sight of the whole. There's nothing more frustrating than drawing a wonderful face, and then finding that the face doesn't fit the figure it's attached to! Working from a simple thumbnail keeps your composition strong and balanced.

STEP TWO: LINE DRAWING

When I moved to the pencil stage, I was actually pretty faithful to the thumbnail. What I typically do is take the thumbnail and enlarge it with a photocopier until it is the size of the art board I'm working on for the final product.

Using a light table – which lights up the art board from behind so that I can see the enlarged thumbnail beneath it – I then pencil the finished drawing, making changes on the fly from the underlying sketch. For instance, I brought Giselle's hair forward to balance the picture. It felt like she was leaning too much to the left, so I added more hair to the right of her face to make the figure feel more balanced. I also simplified the background design.

As you flesh out certain areas, it becomes obvious when you step back that other areas need to be refined. You have to remember to step back. The challenge is to not become so obsessed with the individual pieces that you lose the effect they have on the whole.

Some artists start with a very clear image in their head and strive to recreate that with their art. I tend to be more of a constructive artist, which means I build and modify the image I actually see on the paper – strengthening what I like and erasing what I don't – until I have a satisfactory image. I don't have a "final destination" in mind when I sit down to work. I just roughly know I'm heading west, and see how far I can go in that direction.

That's why the pencil stage is the most creative. It's also the freest stage after thumbnails, because the pencil image restricts everything that follows – even in computer rendering, where it's easy to erase.

STEP THREE: UNDER-PAINTING

Below is the under-painting, where I roughed in the color. You rough in color for the same reason you do a thumbnail – balance. I want my colors to work well together and not look garish or fragment the piece. In the end you want to feel that the color works as a whole, which is just as important as making your figures work together in the same space.

The first impression someone sees in a piece of art is how it works as a whole. Then they focus on smaller individual areas. For example, take a look at a house. Is the overall shape and color nice? If it is, then you notice the color of the trim, or how the shutters set off the siding. It's the same with a paint-ing: If you don't capture the viewer's interest with the piece as a whole, they won't notice the small intricacies that eat up the majority of your time!

With the colors that I chose, my goal was to duplicate that muted palette prevalent in much of art nouveau. The colors aren't terribly bright, but they *seem* bright when placed next to other colors in that palette. It works because of how the eye hunts for contrast.

The colors that were determined before I started the piece are her costume colors, which are purples and golds. Thus, I had that limitation when choosing the background colors. I chose complimentary colors of oranges, blues, and greens, because we know from color theory these work well with the purples and yellows of her costume.

One of the biggest identifying features of art nouveau artwork is a fairly de-saturated look. You achieve that by using colors that are not bright and various shades of just a few colors.

You'll notice that there are only three colors on this piece. There's green going from a yellow-green to a blue-green. There's an orange going from a yellow-orange to a red-orange. And then there is purple going from a lighter red-purple to a deeper blue-purple.

One of the things I realized in the under-painting was that the pencil lines I had drawn on certain features of her face were too harsh, so I ended up removing them. That happens sometimes, and it's one of the things I love about painting digitally. It is not impossible to modify something done in an initial step at the end of the process, unlike "real" painting.

One thing that has come about with digital painting is a wealth of filters, modifiers and tools that imitate "real" paint and drawing. It's very tempting to try to use all those tools and show off. I find that I get the best results by limiting myself to one or two filters per piece, as it forces me to concentrate on the final image and not how I get there.

I used primarily the pencil tool (not the brush!) in Photoshop, which gives a harder, more painterly edge to the color. Obviously, I didn't concentrate on precision, because oil paintings aren't precise. Paint mixes in areas unexpectedly and this is part of the charm of working in oil paint.

The working process for a digital painting is similar to the process for a real painting. You usually start with one color that underlies the piece and you build your major areas slowly up from that, sometimes messily, and then focus on refining small areas of detail. As I duplicate this technique digitally, it evokes the feeling of real paint. There are shortcuts, but a computer can't replace an artist's decisions. The work still needs to be done, but instead of a brush you use a mouse (or, in this case, a stylus).

STEP FOUR: FINAL PAINTING

At the point where I begin the final cover, the under-painting and pencils are two separate pieces. Photoshop is software used for image editing, allowing you to extract or combine images. That's what I chose to do, overlaying the pencil on top of the color to create a third image. As I did this, I thought the pencil art dominated too much in certain areas, like in Giselle's drapery. To get around that, I chose to give the pencil art a color, in effect creating purple lines instead of black lines. This blended better with the paint and created a feeling of cohesion.

Computer coloring is traditionally about hiding the tools you use to make the color. Painting, on the other hand, embraces the brush strokes and the tools used to make the final image. So I left in many of my "mistakes" that I could have fixed. They didn't hurt the image, but enhanced the painterly feel of the final piece.

Giselle's face is the focus of the piece because the color lines radiating from her hand center on her eyes, the border has triangles of gold which all point to her face, and her arm and body position create a pyramid with her face at the apex. The lighting scheme in general highlights her face, as the light is from the top and the lower figure diminishes into darkness.

Her face is the area of the highest detail. One of the things you do in art is spend *your* time where people will spend *their* time. They won't notice the tiny tree in the background, but they will notice whether the face of the foreground figure is beautiful. Knowing this, I spent a good portion of my time making subtle color and drawing changes until I felt the face evoked the expression that I was trying to get across.

The art nouveau aspect I ended up duplicating in the piece is a look that many of Mucha's women presented. There is a subtle smile, a certain gentleness, and a look of contemplation in their

faces. They're not overjoyed. They're not angry. They seem to be pleasantly bemused, if not a little melancholy. For Giselle, I lean toward the bemused…

One thing I've learned is that even with comic art veterans there's no such thing as a free lunch. Don't let your tools fool you. Don't think that the tools are going to do the work for you. You still have a job to do as an artist, even with Photoshop. If you wish to achieve a truly painted look, you need to paint the image totally. Yes, there are programs and filters that can take a photograph and modify it so that it mimics a painted appearance, but it is never, ever perfect, it is ham-fisted, and it usually requires more time to achieve a painted look than if you would have painted from the beginning.